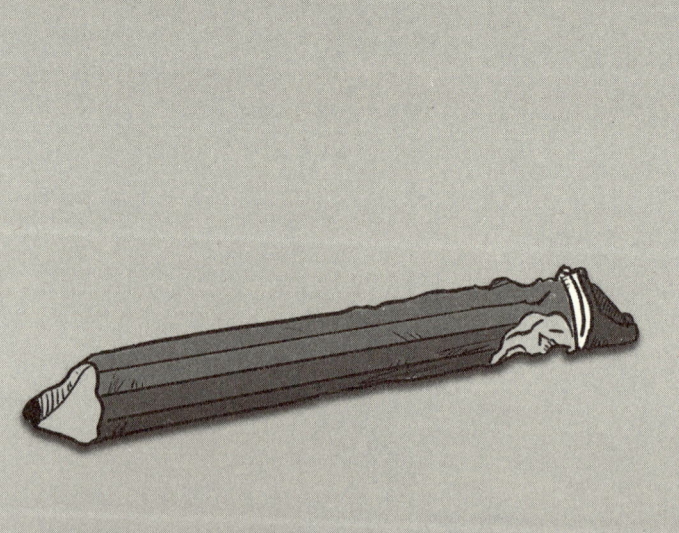

LANA BUTTON

ILLUSTRATED BY SUHARU OGAWA

ORCA BOOK PUBLISHERS

Text copyright © Lana Button 2025
Illustrations copyright © Suharu Ogawa 2025

Published in Canada and the United States in 2025 by Orca Book Publishers.
orcabook.com

All rights are reserved, including those for text and data mining, AI training and similar technologies. No part of this publication may be reproduced or transmitted in any form or by any means, electronic or mechanical, including photocopying, recording or by any information storage and retrieval system now known or to be invented, without permission in writing from the publisher. The publisher expressly prohibits the use of this work in connection with the development of any software program, including, without limitation, training a machine-learning or generative artificial intelligence (AI) system.

Library and Archives Canada Cataloguing in Publication
Title: Brianna Banana, helper of the day / Lana Button ; illustrated by Suharu Ogawa.
Names: Button, Lana, 1968- author. | Ogawa, Suharu, 1979- illustrator.
Series: Orca echoes.
Description: Series statement: Orca echoes
Identifiers: Canadiana (print) 2024034586X | Canadiana (ebook) 20240345886 |
ISBN 9781459840010 (softcover) | ISBN 9781459840027 (PDF) |
ISBN 9781459840034 (EPUB)
Subjects: LCGFT: Novels.
Classification: LCC PS8603.U87 B75 2025 | DDC jC813/.6—dc23

Library of Congress Control Number: 2024934926

Summary: In this illustrated early chapter book, Brianna is convinced she will finally make a friend in her class if she is chosen to be classroom helper, but the new girl, Rumi, is picked instead.

Orca Book Publishers is committed to reducing the consumption of nonrenewable resources in the production of our books. We make every effort to use materials that support a sustainable future.

Orca Book Publishers gratefully acknowledges the support for its publishing programs provided by the following agencies: the Government of Canada, the Canada Council for the Arts and the Province of British Columbia through the BC Arts Council and the Book Publishing Tax Credit.

Cover and interior artwork by Suharu Ogawa.
Design by Troy Cunningham.
Edited by Vanessa McCumber.

Printed and bound in Canada.

28 27 26 25 • 1 2 3 4

*To my friend Sharon McKay
who insisted that I keep going.*

Not Brianna Banana

"Brianna Banana, we are going to be late!" says Grade 8 Lily. She is way up the street. She has stopped again to put her hands on her hips at me. "You need to hurry!"

"I AM!" I yell. Lots of kids walk up Princess Street to get to school. But I am the only one who walks in the ditch. I am sunk right up to my knees in leaves. And I am kicking at them like they are waves at the beach. And that is fun, I tell you. Because what I love is:

1. Leaf kicking.

And what I don't love is:

1. Living on Princess Street.
2. Having zero friends in room 109.
3. Getting in trouble every single day of grade 3. (Nanny would like to know how a kid manages to get into so much trouble when school has just barely started. And I don't have an answer for that woman.)

Plus I can't walk fast because I am also wishing very hard inside my head. And hard wishing slows you down.
Please *me* be *Helper* of the *Day*.
Leaf kicking makes a wish work better, probably. And I *need* to be Helper of the

Day. Then I will have my best day in grade 3, probably. So far grade 3 has been as stinky as old cat farts. (I know this because my nanny has a cat. And his farts will clear a room, I tell you.)

"Brianna Banana!" Grade 8 Lily has stopped again. She is rolling her eyes at me. Lily does not kick leaves. She does not like leaf crumples in her socks, I think. What Grade 8 Lily does like is:

1. Wearing eyeliner.
2. Looking at her phone.
3. Getting to school early.

Lily told me—*in confidence*—that in grade 8, the morning is "prime social time." (When I asked my mom what the heck that is supposed to mean, she said it is teenager talk for "I like to play with my friends." And my nanny said, "That sounds like they are up to no good.")

Grade Eight *playing* is just leaning against the wall with the rest of those big eyeliner kids.

Little kids are not allowed on their side of the school. That is fine by me. Some of those eighth graders are so big they scare the bejeepers out of me.

But my Grade 8 Lily is nice. Nanny gives her money to walk me to school. So being nice is part of the deal, I think.

My mom tells me to follow Lily, even though I am almost nine years old and school is super close to Nanny's. That's where me and Mom have to live now.

I used to take the bus to school. That was when I lived out in Upper Mills with Mom and Dad. We lived in a trailer. And life was simple, I tell you. But then my dad went way out west to find a job. And, super sad news, he found one. And I don't even know when that man is coming back.

My nanny's house is in town. She says our trailer was "way up in the puckerbrush." And Kinsley in my class says that if you live in a trailer, you are trash. That's a bunch of baloney. I didn't feel like trash in my trailer. Now I live on Princess Street. And I don't even feel like a princess.

My grampie died in the summer, and my nanny was super sad. That's why me and Mom had to move here, probably. And so in my family the boys are gone, and the girls live on Princess Street.

This street is super lonely. It's only got old people. Plus Grade 8 Lily. But I won't be lonely when I am Helper of the Day.

Because then, I bet, kids in my class will do two things:

1. Play with me.
2. Stop calling me Brianna Banana.

My mom says everyone calls me Brianna Banana because it is a fun name to say. That is because her name is regular. And doesn't rhyme with fruit.

But I don't just rhyme with a banana. I look like one. If everyone in my class is like a regular-size apple, then I'm the tallest banana. When I get in trouble (like I've done a gazillion bazillion times so far in grade 3), my head pokes up way higher than everyone else's head. And I stand out like a rotten banana.

Plus my hair is yellow and as slippy as a banana peel. Ponytails slide right out, no matter how tight I twist them. That's probably why no one in my class wants to play with me.

My mom says, "Be a friend to make a friend." Like that is some kind of magic trick. It doesn't even make sense. I am the friendliest friend the grade 3 class ever met!

That's when I hear, "Watch out!"

Andrew and Markus from my class whiz up the sidewalk on scooters. They are doing show-off scooter zigzags at me. Andrew thinks he is a smarty-pants because he says everything in grade 3 is easy-peasy. And my nanny calls Markus a smart aleck because he says mean things just to be funny. Markus calls out, "Don't slip on that Brianna Banana!"

And I hate that! I hate it more than Nanny's pork stew.

Mom says, "Don't react." She says it's more fun to tease me if I do. She says, "Ignore them, and they'll stop." I think Mom is too old to remember grade 3. Because her plan never works.

So before I go back to wishing about being Helper of the Day, and having lots of friends, I think up my own mean names to yell. "Hey, watch yourself, Andrew Apple Pants, and...and...Markus Poopy Potato!" I chuck a handful of slimy leaves at them.

Too bad for me, that handful of leaves is hiding a rock. And that rock clocks Markus right in the back of his poopy potato head.

Wishing with Leslie

"Brianna Banana! What did you do now?" Grade 8 Lily stomps back down the street toward me. Markus and Andrew have stopped, and Markus is holding the back of his head.

"Sorry!" I yell at Markus. Because I am sorry. Not about the slimy-leaves part. But I didn't mean to throw that sneaky rock. And I hope his head is okay.

But good news—no blood! And not a teacher in sight! Markus does not want to look like a crybaby in front of Andrew, probably. So he gets back on his scooter and whizzes away. But first he holds up his middle finger at me, which is rude, I tell you.

Lily is looking like she has just about had enough of me. So I decide I am tired of leaf kicking. I hustle-walk up Princess Street.

And we are not even late! We get to school right when my old bus pulls up. Lily heads straight for the eyeliner crowd. I wait for Leslie.

Leslie is the little second grader I used to sit with on the bus. He's got his own name problems. Kids say he's got a girl's name. Leslie is quiet and scared-ish when kids say mean things. Like when they call him "girlie-boy" or ask him, "When is the flood?" (My mom says that is a mean tease to say when someone has grown too

tall for their pants but has to wear them anyway.) I did all the yelling for Leslie. But now I am a walk-to-schooler, so my bus-yelling days are over.

"Hi, Leslie."

"Hi, Brianna."

"I bet I'm Helper of the Day today, Leslie," I say as we head to the playground.

"You bet that every day," he says.

"I know I bet that every day, Leslie. But it has to be my turn soon!" I say. "Nearly everyone in my class has been helper. They already got to—" I hold my fingers up and count at Leslie.

"One. Sit in Mrs. Newberry's really special helper's chair."

Leslie nods in agreement.

"Two. Hold Mrs. Newberry's doughnut-shaped pointer stick."

"Mm-hmm." Leslie nods again.

"And three. All the other helper things!" I wave my fingers in excitement. "Like be line leader, and pass out papers, and—**best part**—go *upstairs* to deliver the library books!"

"Fun," Leslie says.

"Yes, fun!" I say. "Third graders hardly ever go upstairs. So that is mysterious and exciting, probably."

"Yeah," he says.

"Because Grade 8 Lily told me—*in confidence*—that upstairs doesn't just have our library, it has—" I get ready to count at Leslie again.

"One. A CHEMISTRY lab!

"Two. Lockers with actual LOCKS!

"And three..." I clear my throat and lower my voice. "Grade 8 bathrooms where you reapply eyeliner and cheek-defining bronzer. *And* deodorant! And that is why little kids can't go up there *unaccompanied*, probably."

"Probably." Leslie nods his head quietly.

"When you are the helper, everyone pretends to *like* you," I remind Leslie.

"Yup," he agrees.

"Because you get to pick a friend to go *with* you to the library."

"Mm-hmm." Leslie nods again.

"None of those helpers have ever picked me, Leslie," I say.

"No fair," he says.

"I know that is no fair. But when *I* am Helper of the Day, I will see for myself how that book delivery goes. And today is probably the day!" I say, very excited. "Make a wish with me, Leslie!" I grab his hands.

"We do this every morning, Brianna," Leslie complains.

"Hurry up!" I command. "We need to wish before the bell rings or it won't work, probably," I say.

"Fine," Leslie says. He rolls his eyes before he shuts them.

I wish hard, out loud. "Please, oh please, let me be Helper of the Day."

"Yeah, please, please let her," Leslie says, fast and quiet so no one hears.

We get that wishing done just when the bell goes. Kids are getting into their lines.

"I probably can't do any yelling for you at recess," I yell at Leslie from my line. "Because if I'm Helper of the Day, I will be way too busy."

"Uh-huh." Leslie nods at me as the second graders walk inside.

I smile at that hope. Today will probably be my best day in grade 3. Everyone in my class will want to play with me. I bet everyone in that whole room will want to be my friend. And no one will dare call me Brianna Banana.

Coats for Breakfast

When you are Helper of the Day, you know right away. It says it on the whiteboard. Plus kids shout your name. And they run to you like you are an important grade 3 bigwig.

I stay in the hallway and listen. So far I do not hear name shouting. I just hear my heart thumping. I shove myself right inside my locker for one more wish.

Locker time in the morning is the fresh start to your whole school day. You haven't

gotten in any trouble yet. My mom says some days start off on the wrong foot. But that won't happen when I am the helper. I stuff my face in my jacket fluff so no one hears my "please, please, please" wish.

"Brianna Banana!" Kinsley says loud so that all the kids look. "Are you *eating* your coat?"

Kinsley is the girl in my class with all the friends—except for me. She is also the leader of the Cheese Girls. That is the group of girls in my class who play together. I am not a member. I don't even know why they are called Cheese Girls. The reason is kept top secret, I think.

"*Ew*, Brianna Banana, that's *gross*!" Clare says loud and squealy. Clare is the second in command of the Cheese Girls. I think that is because she is a big copier of whatever Kinsley does.

"Brianna, do you eat *coats* for breakfast?" Clare says. She does a laugh right at my face, like she is the funniest Cheese Girl in the world. "Does it *taste* good?"

"Wow, Clare," I say, super mad. "Your breath smells like you ate *poop* for breakfast!" And because I'm still mad, I yell, "Which makes you the biggest-ever **Poop Face**!" Those mean words go right out of my mouth and down the hallway before I have time to think about it.

Thinking about it, and taking belly breaths, is what I'm supposed to do when I get mad. But my mad happens so fast, I don't usually make it. *After* is when I remember all that breathing, walking-away stuff. And once you say them, you can't gobble mean words back up.

And here is the thing about mean words. Grown-ups have ears like a hawk for that kind of stuff. The word *poop* shoots right down the hall...right into the ears of our principal, Mr. Tilly.

"Who said that?!" he shouts.

More Bad Names

Mr. Tilly is the tallest man I know. Plus he wears an important suit every day. His shiny tie-up shoes make a clicking sound on the hallway floors. Mr. Tilly stops in his shiny-shoe tracks and roars, "*Who* is being rude?"

That loud hallway goes silent, I tell you. Kids freeze like in a game of freeze tag. They make their faces look shocked as if to say *I have never said* poop *in my whole entire life.* And then everyone's eyeballs slide to me.

Mr. Tilly sees me, and his lips press in tight. He and I know each other. We've talked a couple times this year.

I have mostly climbed back inside my locker. My face is shoved back into my coat fluff. I am wishing *super hard* that Mr. Tilly will let this one go.

He leans his head into my locker, so all those nosy kids can't hear. "We don't want to start our day off like this, do we, Miss Ross?"

My whole name is Brianna (not Banana) Ross. When Mr. Tilly calls me Miss Ross, it is not a good sign.

I take my face away from my coat to show him I am doing a really big belly breath. That is the breath he taught me for calming down. Sometimes we go for walks up and down the hallway. We practice doing them when I need a brain break

from grade 3. And we are getting pretty good at them.

But this time I clamp my eyes shut and make my face look very serious. I do a big breath in and a big breath out. And, lucky me, I do it so good he walks away.

This day is not on the right foot so far. My face needs to stop being so hot.

Markus will call me Brianna the Burned-Up Banana.

I wait for the commotion to wind down. And for kids to mind their own beeswax. Then I walk into room 109.

Everyone is rushing to Rumi.

Rumi moved new to our school this year. In fact, she moved new to our whole entire country. My nanny says she's "from away." That must be pretty far.

Rumi is in my grade 3 class even though she is as tall as a kindergartener. And I have not heard that kid talk one bit. My nanny says if you are a squeaky wheel, you get attention. Rumi is the quietest wheel in our class. And so some days I forget she is there. But now all the kids are patting Rumi's back like she is a superstar.

And just like that, I know the Helper of the Day…is not me.

Not the Helper

Kids cheer at Rumi. And they push to stand close to her. Rumi is hugging her arms tight, like she is being squished by this brand-new attention.

"Rumi, your shirt is *so* pretty," Clare says. She says this even though Rumi's shirt is just plain blue. And it doesn't have sparkles or glitter, which are Clare's favorite kinds of fabric. Clare is being a big faker, I think.

"Rumi, I love what you do to your hair," says one of the nice Cheese Girls, named Lara. But Rumi's hair is just the same short black hair she always has.

I sure wish those girls fussed over me like that. But this kid is looking like a Gloomy Rumi.

And she just stays quiet, even when five people say, "Come to my birthday."

Then Daniel says, "You can play with me at recess."

But Kinsley slides right between Daniel and Rumi. "Don't be *ridiculous*," Kinsley says. "She's going to play with *us*."

What? Kinsley only plays with Cheese Girls! But she puts her arm around Rumi like they have been pals all this time.

And Rumi does not even look excited. My nanny would say Rumi's scared stiff.

Her eyes are ginormous wide, like a mouse trapped in a corner.

"*We*" —Kinsley points to herself while the other girls jam behind her— "are the Cheese Girls. And *we* do lots of super-fun things at recess. And *we* would like you to join us—just for today."

Wow! Those Cheese Girls *never* let *me* play! They told me their membership has been full since kindergarten! And no new members—probably until grade 5! What a bunch of cheesy liars!

Then Markus says to Kinsley, "You're just saying that so she picks you to deliver the books."

Markus goes to the other side of Rumi. "Hey, Ronnie, you can hang out with me," he says. "I'll make sure you get those books to the library safe and sound."

Rumi's scared-mouse eyes ping-pong between these arguing kids.

"Her name isn't Ronnnnnnie!" Clare squeals at Markus. "It's *Julie*." She rolls her eyes like she is a teenager.

These nincompoops are starting to drive me bonkers. They don't even notice Rumi's big, mousy eyes filling all the way up with tears. I gotta set this little mouse free.

"HEY!" I bark in their faces. "The kid's name is *Rumi*. Now give her some air!"

Then we hear Mrs. Newberry sing, "Good morning, everyone. It's time to start our day." Our teacher starts every single day of grade 3 like that. It's babyish. But I kind of love it because Mrs. Newberry looks so darn happy to see us.

Mrs. Newberry has been teaching for so long, she was *my mom's* grade 3 teacher! So she is super old but really good at grade 3. She knows how to teach *and* be nice.

Mrs. Newberry takes Rumi to the helper's chair. It is the fanciest chair in the history of chairs, probably. I think it is an antique from when my mom was in grade 3. The other chairs at our desks are blue and normal plastic. But the helper's chair is shiny red and wooden. It's super smooth on your bum, probably. When you are Helper of the Day, you sit there while the rest of us stare at you from the boring carpet. And you look like the boss of grade 3!

Rumi is such a lucky duck on that helper's chair. But she looks like she wants to hide. I decide to cheer her on by yelling, "Looking good up there, Rumi!"

Mrs. Newberry reminds me about not shouting out at morning meeting. So I give Rumi a big, quiet thumbs-up while

Mr. Tilly's voice comes over the loudspeaker to talk and talk about announcements.

Then, boy oh boy, when Mrs. Newberry brings out that fantastic doughnut pointer stick, Rumi sure changes her glum tune. She takes that pointer with both hands and points to our daily schedule like it might do magic. I feel super happy for that kid! And lucky Rumi, when we skip-count numbers on the calendar, she gets to point all the way to the end of September, because that is what day we are on.

"That pointer stick sure feels sturdy and smooth, I bet! Huh, Rumi?"

"Quiet, please, Brianna. Let's count with Rumi," Mrs. Newberry says.

But skip-counting by threes doesn't make any sense in my head. So I shout out, "Don't you just love that pointer?"

"Please count along, Brianna," Mrs. Newberry says.

When morning meeting is done, Rumi looks happy to give Mrs. Newberry back her pointer.

While everyone is getting up from the carpet and going to their tables I go over and pat Rumi on the back. "Great job, Rumi!" I say.

And guess what? She smiles—right at me! Kind of like a happy little mouse. And...kind of like a friend! Wow! That gives me an idea!

A Friend Idea

This new kid probably needs someone to do yelling for her. And I am *great* at yelling. So maybe Rumi and I could be real-life friends in room 109!

Mrs. Newberry talks on and on, saying something like "pay attention, please." And so it is hard for me to concentrate on my plan. And I want to tell Rumi about it right now!

"Hey, Rumi! Over here, Rumi!" I whisper-yell to her table across the room.

Rumi is distracted by all of Mrs. Newberry's teaching. She just keeps paying attention to the teacher and not me.

So I whisper-yell a little louder, "Want to talk at recess, Rumi?" I smile my friendliest smile. "Recess is *prime social time*!" I try to get her to see me winking. "I can be a big helper to you, probably."

"Shhhhh, Brianna Banana, I can't *hear*," Kinsley says, super mean. She and I have been sitting right beside each other since grade 3 started. It is called *assigned seating*. That means you sit beside someone, like it or lump it. I don't think it is one of Mrs. Newberry's best ideas. Kinsley is supposed to be my elbow partner, but she is like my elbow enemy.

I ignore her and try again to get Rumi's attention. I swing my arms big in the air to make her look. "Rumi! I play a

really fun game called soft sand at recess. Wanna play?"

She is still not looking, so that makes me say louder, **"I PLAY WITH THIS BOY NAMED LESLIE BUT HE'S STILL A BOY AND YOU CAN PLAY TOO!"**

Then Mrs. Newberry shushes a warning shush at me, like she has just about had enough. My nanny says I can play right on your very last nerve. And make you blow your top. I don't want Mrs. Newberry to blow her top and say, "We should have a little talk at recess." So I take one of those belly breaths and put my arms down.

"Can the Helper of the Day please pass out the worksheets?" Mrs. Newberry asks. She hands Rumi a pile.

Rumi mostly has her head down as she walks to each table. But at my table she shocks the bejeepers out of me because:

1. She peeks—right at me.
2. She has a bit of twinkling in her shy eyes.
3. She does a friendly little smile! Just to *me*!

So I make a big wish that Rumi and I *will* play at recess. Like real friends. Best friends! **Besties!!!**

Then Mrs. Newberry says something about "now you know what to do."

I look down at the paper Rumi gave me. *Hmmmmm.* My brain lets out a sigh. Because...what the heck is this?

"You should have lots of time to finish before first recess," says Mrs. Newberry. "Let's quietly get to work."

Uh-oh.

Scribbling Mad

So here's the thing. I am going to guess that while I was busy planning about Rumi being my friend, Mrs. Newberry talked with everybody else about this confusing paper, probably. And I didn't actually catch any of that.

I do a big *I don't know what to do* sigh. And then I say, "I don't get this paper one bit." But no one at my table comes to my rescue. Andrew Apple Pants, who sits across from me, is printing away.

He is dancing his head side to side. He is smiling like he has a mouth full of easy-peasy lemon-squeezy pie. And that is annoying, I tell you. Lara the nice Cheese Girl is the other kid across from me. She is also acting suspiciously like nothing hard is going on around here.

The room is so super quiet, my ears hum.

But I am too panicky to mention my confusing paper to Mrs. Newberry. Because she might ask, "Were you paying attention?" You've got to watch out for that sneaky trick question. I have fallen for it a few times. If I tell on myself and say I wasn't listening to her, Mrs. Newberry's friendly teacher eyes will look disappointed at me. And I hate that.

So that is why I take matters into my own hands. And I just leeeeean over a

bit...to take...a little look...at my elbow enemy's paper.

Kinsley's printing is always perfect. Probably because of her fancy-pants glitter pencil. That thing has distracting sparkles, I tell you. The eraser is shaped like a diamond. Kinsley never even uses that diamond eraser. Because she never makes

mistakes. Her printing comes out super neat and in all the right shapes on her first try.

My yellow pencil is stubby. The eraser fell out. Plus there are chew marks on it. So it makes my printing come out dark and smudgy. When grade 3 first started, Kinsley said I print like I am in kindergarten. And that made me shove her off her seat.

Sometimes when I get mad, I don't even know my own strength, I tell you. Kinsley landed right on her keister. That is my nanny's way of saying "she fell on her butt."

And I'll tell you what, they don't put up with shoving shenanigans in grade 3.

That was my first time taking a belly-breathing walk with Mr. Tilly.

With her super-neat printing, Kinsley has made exact round circles around some words on her paper. And she has filled in lots of blanks with other words.

I lean over to get a better look. I can hardly make out what the heck this kid is doing. Then she surprises the bejeepers out of me! "Stop COPYING me, Brianna Banana!" she yells.

"I'm NOT copying!" I yell back. "I am just **LOOKING** at what you are **DOING!**" I roll my eyes at her.

"**THAT'S COPYING!!**" Kinsley shouts, so shocked and mad.

Mrs. Newberry stands up from her desk and stares a laser beam at me. "Do you need a break, Brianna?" Her voice is friendly, but her lips are not smiling.

Plus her eyes are giving me a warning. Most of the day Mrs. Newberry's whole face smiles. So when it doesn't, it stops you right in your tracks.

I answer by moving to my side of the table. I make my eyes stare big and bulgy at my confusing paper. I wiggle my head side to side like I think it's easy-peasy. And I stay like that until Mrs. Newberry sits back down.

Kinsley folds her arms over her paper like she is hiding treasure. "Copying is *cheating*, Brianna Banana. And *cheating* is bad," she says, mean and quiet. "You do bad stuff all the time. That's why no one plays with you."

I feel a stab in my heart. I want to yell that she is the worst elbow enemy in the history of grade 3. But instead I poke my pencil right on her perfect paper. And I make the meanest, hardest scribble I can.

"**AHHH!**" Kinsley yells. "Mrs. Newberry! Mrs. Newberry! She ***scribbled*** on my paper!" Then Kinsley throws her head back and cries like we are in kindergarten. "She **RUINED** it!"

Mrs. Newberry stands up again. Only this time she says, "Brianna, come here, please." Her voice is not messing around.

And that is when the first recess bell rings. Clare and the Cheese Girls rush over to put their arms around Kinsley. Because guess what? That diamond eraser isn't even any good at getting out scribbles.

I watch Rumi head outside by herself. There goes my chance to play with her. Because from the look on Mrs. Newberry's face, I am not going anywhere.

Too Many Coats and Just Enough Soft Sand

I do a lot of belly breathing at first recess. For the rest of the school morning, I manage to "keep my nose clean." That's what Nanny says when I stay out of trouble. I finally get sprung from room 109 at lunch recess.

The playground is stuffed with kids. But I know where to find Leslie. He's at the corner of the school where nobody shoots balls at you.

Leslie hands me a stick from the ones he keeps in his pocket. We sit down together.

We start swishing back the pebbly dirt. And we find the perfect soft sand underneath to start our pile.

I break the news to him. "I am not Helper of the Day, Leslie," I say.

"No fair," Leslie says softly.

"Yeah." I push at the rubbly sand, kind of grouchy. "This new girl Rumi is," I say. "So then the Cheese Girls made her a member. So for sure Rumi will pick Kinsley to deliver the books."

"Sneaky," says Leslie.

"So sneaky of them, Leslie," I say. I take the edge of my stick and slide more soft sand into the pile.

"Is that her?" Leslie asks. He points to Rumi. She is right beside us. Her arms are stuffed with a pile of coats that goes right up to her chin.

"What are you doing?" I ask her.

"Kinsley told me to carry the Cheese Girls' coats," Rumi says from behind the coats. Wow, that is the actual first time I've heard the sound of Rumi's voice. It comes out regular, even though she doesn't use it much.

"I don't want to drop them," she says, leaning against the wall.

The day is a lot hotter from this morning. So I take my coat off too. I even think about adding it to Rumi's pile, so it

doesn't get dusty from soft sand. But then I notice Rumi looks stuffed with coats.

"Yeah, actually, that doesn't sound very fair," I say.

"Yeah, not fair," says Leslie. He is shy with new people, so he is kind of peeking from behind my knee when he says this.

"And maybe you need some help with those." I take the coats and put them in a grassy spot.

Rumi stares at our pile of sand.

"Wanna help us?" I ask.

"Okay," she says.

Leslie gives her a stick, and I show her how to swish it. That kid is a natural at it, I tell you! By the time the bell rings, the three of us have made the biggest pile in soft-sand history!

But then we hear a bossy voice. "*Rumi*! We *need* our coats!!"

Rumi looks at me, panicked.

"Here, hold out your arms," I tell her. I pile those babies up like I am a digger loading a dump truck.

Rumi balances them and stumble-walks quick to the grade 3 line.

And Leslie leaves too.

And just like that, I'm mad. I don't want to stop this fun game.

Everyone but me is doing what they are told and lining up, and Kinsley has grabbed Rumi's hand.

I am never getting in that line. I don't want to be trapped in grade 3 with:

1. No friends.
2. More confusing papers.
3. Rumi picking Kinsley to deliver the library books.

So I don't move a muscle. I don't even budge when the recess teacher yells my name. She waves her pack of pink slips at me like a mean little flag. A pink slip says *Go see Mr. Tilly and tell him you got in trouble at recess.* I've collected a few so far.

I think about how Mr. Tilly would say, "Take a belly breath, Miss Ross." I breathe in. And I breathe out like I am Brianna the Big Bad Wolf. And I stomp to that line. But first I do a big kick and send that soft sand flying.

Rumi's Pick

"Rumi, it is time for you and a friend to deliver the books to the library," says Mrs. Newberry.

This is when everyone does little jumps in the helper's face. They stretch out their arms and whisper-yell, "Pick *me*."

Only Kinsley doesn't do it. She stands back and twinkles her eyes, just waiting to get picked.

I usually stretch and beg the loudest. And it doesn't get me anywhere, I tell you.

I am not even in the mood for that foolishness today. I don't even make a *pick me* wish. I already know that for the rest of this wrong-foot day I will:

1. Not get picked.
2. Not have a friend in sight.
3. Just get in bigger trouble, probably.

I don't even want to watch myself not get picked. So I stick my head glum on my desk. That is why I don't even see what happens next.

"*Who?*" I hear someone say, surprised.

"Who are you picking?" other kids ask.

Then Clare squeals, "You want *Brianna Banana* to go with you?!"

I look up. And Rumi's finger is pointing right at *me*!

"Yaay!" I yell a surprised yell. "Yes! Of course I will help you deliver the books, Rumi!"

I run up and yank at the book bag in Mrs. Newberry's hand. But it won't budge from her strong teacher grip.

Kinsley is tapping Mrs. Newberry. "Should *I* go as well, Mrs. Newberry?" she asks, like she is the sweetest elbow partner grade 3 has ever seen. "I know my way to the library. And *they* don't."

"Yeah, that's because you get picked almost every single time!" I say right in her face. "Only Rumi didn't pick *you*. She picked *me*!"

"Well, *you* are probably going to get *lost*." Kinsley folds her arms at me.

"Mind your own beeswax!" I yell.

Mrs. Newberry looks surprised, like she was not expecting this twist. She leans close to me like we are talking in private. "Brianna," she says kindly, "Rumi is new to our school—"

"And our country," I interrupt helpfully.

Mrs. Newberry takes in a long breath through her nose, then puts her smile back on her face. "Rumi hasn't delivered the books before." She is talking slow, like she is thinking up a plan. "And this is also your first time walking to the library on your own. It can be a bit tricky because it is up on our second floor…in the intermediate wing. Perhaps having a third friend come along could be fun? Just in case you get confused."

Confused. Mrs. Newberry said it with a smile. But it feels worse than a mean tease. Grade 3 is so easy-peasy to everyone else, and I am Brianna the confused banana.

I have to deliver those library books without help. If I don't, Mrs. Newberry will think I am the most confused kid she has ever seen in room 109 since the olden days when she started teaching.

"**NO!** She picked **ME!**" I shout, and I yank so hard that the bag comes free from her hands.

Yelling and yanking at Mrs. Newberry is not recommended. She gives me a warning tilt of her head. I breathe in a big belly breath and let it out like I am blowing out a million birthday candles. And I show her with my eyes that I *can* do this. "I really don't want any help being a friend to Rumi," I say. And I make a *please, please, please* wish inside my head.

"Okay, Brianna," Mrs. Newberry says slowly. And she smiles like she magically heard my wish. And I am so relieved, I wrap my arms around her. And I hug that teacher right there in front of everyone.

Mrs. Newberry opens the door to our classroom and says, "Go straight down this hall." She stops until I look her in the eyes again. Because I am doing a little ants-in-my-pants dance. So I stop and show her how good I'm listening.

"At the *top* of the stairs, turn *right*..." and then she says more stuff. But all my

brain hears is "*Yaay* for me! I am delivering the books today!!!" So I don't actually catch that last part.

I skip out the door, swinging the book bag, super happy.

"Brianna," Mrs. Newberry calls. "Aren't you forgetting something?"

I look back. Rumi is standing in our classroom.

"Right!" I go to grab her. But Rumi isn't budging. She is looking a bit mousy-scared of our hall.

And it doesn't help when Markus pats her shoulder and says, "I bet you get lost and we never see you again."

"Yeah," Kinsley says. "And for sure you will get in trouble. Brianna Banana *always* gets in trouble." She folds her arms, with a sneery face. "*That* is what you get when you don't pick a Cheese Girl."

"Forget those fart faces, Rumi!" I say, yanking at her hand. "You are in the best hands with me." I yank at her some more until her feet start to shuffle.

"We are gonna have the best adventure delivering these books." I try to make her skip, but her feet are walking very cautious. "And when we get back, we will tell all those stinky butts, 'We showed you!'"

I smile at that thought as I stomp us up the stairs. And I whip us around a corner. And I walk us all the way down a hall. And when we turn the next corner, Rumi has even stopped squishing my hand like she wants to get off a Tilt-A-Whirl ride. She is just holding my hand like a friendly friend!

But then I look up. Because, *um*...

"Sheesh," I say. "Who knew this hallway happened at our school?"

I keep walking, but there isn't a library in sight. There are classrooms with big, deodorant-wearing kids sitting at their very own one-person desks.

I fake a smile at Rumi. And I act like I know what to do next. And I pretend that me and the Helper of the Day are not lost. "So." I smile at her. "Where exactly is *from away*?"

Being a Friend

So here is the thing. For my entire school life, getting to the library was easy-peasy. Just follow the line. Because teachers know which corners to turn. So paying attention is not even part of the trip. But now I am teacherless. And I can't figure out what the heck they did with the library.

I do more small talk to Rumi and pretend that Helper of the Day always walks around this weird upstairs hallway (which is off-limits for third graders, probably).

"Thank you for picking me to deliver these books, Rumi," I say.

"Thank you for helping me today," Rumi says.

I look surprised at her. Because I don't know what she is talking about.

"You told everyone how to say my name. And you waved at me when I was scared of sitting in front of the whole class. And you helped me with the coats. And you let me play soft sand."

"Whoa, I *did* do all that!" I say, surprised at myself. "Wow, Rumi! I was a friend—and I made a friend! My mom always says that! And wow oh wow! My mom knew what the heck she was talking about this time!! Because we *are* friends, right, Rumi?"

Rumi smiles. "Right," she says.

"This is the best news!" I dance her in a circle right there in that lost hallway.

And then I grab my friend and turn us around a brand-new corner, very determined. Because I need to get this Helper of the Day to the library!

Mr. Tilly's Keister

Except this new hall is super scary. It is a dead end. Big kids almost as tall as Mr. Tilly come out of classrooms. And there is eyeliner and bronzer as far as the eye can see, I tell you! Teenagers stomp like giants and slam lockers. Rumi and I hold hands very tight with fear.

And then I feel a ruffle on my head. "Brianna Banana, what are *you* doing in the *grade 8* hallway?"

Look who it is! My walk-to-school Grade 8 Lily! And I don't even mind that she called me Brianna Banana! Because am I ever glad to see her!

"Lily!" I hug her legs.

She and the big teenagers have leaned over Rumi and me, acting like we are puppies. And they make "Ohhhh" sounds at us.

"Soooo cute! Are you Helper of the Day, Brianna Banana?"

"Rumi is," I tell her.

And those teenagers make more "Ohhhh" sounds and say, "Hi, Rumi."

And this time Rumi looks like she doesn't even mind getting fussed at.

"Ohhhh, I remember being Helper of the Day!!" The big kids coo some more.

"Are you taking the books to the library?" Lily asks.

I nod yes. Then Lily and those eighth graders take us back down a hall, away

from all that racket. They turn us around a corner. And look at that! The library! It is on the wrong side of where it is supposed to be, but there it is!

"Thank you!" I say to Lily and the eyeliner crowd.

"Come on!" I yank Rumi into a run. "Let's get these books delivered!"

But, too bad for us, I am looking at Rumi and running us both super fast. So that is why I don't see Mr. Tilly until it is too late.

He is standing right up on his tippy-toes. He is putting something on a bulletin board. And he is not even looking out for runaway kids. And that is why we crash right into Mr. Tilly. And that is how, by accident, I knock the principal right on his keister. And that guy goes down like a ton of bricks, I tell you.

"MISS ROSS!" Mr. Tilly roars from the floor.

I fake-smile at Rumi like we are not in big trouble. But my nanny would say, "Young lady, your Helper-of-the-Day goose is cooked."

Delivered

So far in grade 3, I have:

1. Missed recess a gazillion times.
2. Got pink slips.
3. Walked miles up and down the hall doing belly breaths.

But this is the very first time I have knocked the principal on his butt. My nanny is going to blow her top when she hears about this. It is the biggest crime in the history of grade 3, probably.

"Mr. Tilly! I am so sorry!" While I yank him back to his feet, I explain very loud and fast, "We are delivering the library books! Only the library was nowhere to be found!

"And then we were almost trampled by a rowdy crowd of teenagers—who should know better." I wave my finger at him. "You might want to get control of that situation." I point to where Rumi and I came from. "Down that spooky hallway no one told me about."

Mr. Tilly brushes off his important suit and sighs with a pretend smile on his face. "*This* is why we don't run in the hall, Miss Ross and…?" He looks at Rumi.

"Rumi," I say, trying to change the running subject. "She is new to our school *and* our country *and* she is Helper of the Day **and** she picked **ME** to deliver the books with her!!" I take a breath. "Because *you'll never guess what*, Mr. Tilly! I was a friend and I made a friend, just like my mom said!"

"I am happy to hear that," Mr. Tilly says. This time he smiles like he means it.

I pick up the bulletin-board pieces that went flying. "Want help?" I ask.

And wow, Mr. Tilly lets Rumi and me hand him pieces while he finishes the bulletin board!

Then Mr. Tilly holds open the library door and waits while we put the books on the librarian's desk. She is nowhere in sight and the place is deserted. It is so super quiet in that room, my ears ring. So I scoot Rumi out of there very fast.

"I happen to be heading toward your class right now," Mr. Tilly says. "Why don't we walk together?" he asks.

"Oh, sure," I say, like it is no big deal. But I am glad at this coincidence. I have actually had enough of trespassing in these big-kid hallways for one day.

Quick as a wink we see room 109. And that is a welcome sight, I tell you!

"There it is!" I yank Rumi into a run. But then I hear Mr. Tilly clear his great big throat. So I slow my feet. And I walk my friend right into our class.

Best Day Ever in Grade 3

"There you are!" Mrs. Newberry says. "Did everything go okay?" she asks.

Everyone is working at their desks. They look at me and Rumi like we have been gone for forty years.

That's when Mr. Tilly pokes his head in.

"Excuse me, Mrs. Newberry, can I see you for a second?" he asks.

Just before Mrs. Newberry steps into the hallway, she says, "Okay, my friends, please start your silent reading."

But instead of taking out his book and minding his own beeswax, Markus points to me and Rumi. "*You're* in *trouble*!!" He sings it like it is a mean song.

"I knew you'd do something bad," says Clare.

"And I bet Mr. Tilly caught you. Didn't he!" Kinsley says with the meanest cheesy smile.

And I think that the answer is yes. And I think maybe Rumi does not want to be friends with someone that:

1. Gets lost.
2. Gets confused.
3. Gets in trouble.
4. Looks like a banana.

So I stop holding her hand.

But Rumi just grabs my hand right back. And she says right to Kinsley, with her own, hardly-ever-used voice, "Brianna showed me the grade 8 hallway."

Kinsley looks jealous.

"And eighth graders talked to us," Rumi says. "It was fun."

Clare folds her arms in a huff.

And then Mrs. Newberry comes back inside.

"Miss Ross," Mr. Tilly says, from the door, loud so everyone can hear, "thank you for introducing me to your friend Rumi. And thank you both for helping me with the bulletin board."

And I feel like I might burst with pride and happiness. That is the first time in the history of being called Miss Ross that I am not even in trouble!

Rumi does a shy look at me. So I answer for both of us with a booming, "You're welcome, Mr. Tilly!" And then I add, like he and I are old pals, "I hope your keister is okay!"

Markus and Kinsley and Clare have their mouths hanging open in shock. But other kids, like Lara and Daniel, smile as if they are impressed with me. And what do you know, Andrew Apple Pants even gives me a thumbs-up.

And then, right before Rumi goes to her seat, she whispers in my ear.

And I smile the biggest smile in the history of my grade 3 life. It is a wish-come-true smile!

I can't wait to tell Leslie that you can have your best day in grade 3 without being Helper of the Day. Because Rumi called me her bestie! And she didn't even call me Brianna Banana.

MORE ORCA ECHOES!

Twins Henry and Allie buy their mom a pair of headphones for her work-from-home meetings, but they soon discover something much better: an empty room in the basement that they can make into her very own office!

When eleven-year-old Hailey and her friend Kyle make a wish on a Chinese lion statue, they accidentally bring a dragon to life. Now they must find a way to help her get home.

Bailey is nervous about their first day at the Hero Academy, an elementary school for young superheroes. Can Bailey fit in when surrounded by classmates with incredible powers?

IAN CRYSLER

Lana Button is an early childhood educator and the author of more than a dozen books for children, including *Stay My Baby*, *Tough Like Mum* and the Kitty and Friends series. Her books have been shortlisted for the Blue Spruce Award, Shining Willow Award, IODE Jean Throop Book Award and Rainforest of Reading, and they have been recognized as Canadian Children's Book Centre's Best Books and an IBBY Outstanding Book for Young Children. Lana is a former actress who considers every read-aloud a mini performance. When not writing new stories, Lana spends her time traveling to schools and festivals to share her passion for social-emotional literacy. She lives in Burlington, Ontario.

DARCY MacQUARRIE

Suharu Ogawa is a Toronto-based illustrator. Her love for drawing started in a kindergarten art school after being kicked out of calligraphy class for refusing to convert to right-handedness. Formally trained in art history and cultural anthropology, she worked for several years as a university librarian until her passion for illustration called her out of that career and into the pursuit of a lifelong dream. Since then, Suharu has created illustrations for magazines, public art projects and children's books, including *All Consuming: Shop Smarter for the Planet*, *Cities: How Humans Live Together* and *Why Humans Work: How Jobs Shape Our Lives and Our World*. She also teaches illustration at OCAD University in Toronto.